MARY HOFFMAN has written around 90 books for children
and in 1998 was made an Honorary Fellow of the Library Association
for services to children and libraries. She is also the editor of the online
quarterly children's book review *Armadillo*. In 1992 her book *Amazing Grace*
was selected for Children's Book of the Year, commended for the
Kate Greenaway Medal and added to the National Curriculum Reading List,
becoming an international bestseller. It was followed by *Grace & family*, *Princess Grace*
and three Grace story books: *Starring Grace*, *Encore, Grace!* and *Bravo, Grace!*
Mary's many other books for Frances Lincoln include *The Colour of Home*,
Seven Wonders of the Ancient World and *Three Wise Women*.
Mary lives near Oxford.

Find out more at www.maryhoffman.co.uk

CORNELIUS VAN WRIGHT's and YING-HWA HU's books include
Make a Joyful Sound, *Sam and the Lucky Money*,
Zora Hurston and the Chinaberry Tree
and, with Mary Hoffman, *Princess Grace*.
They live in New York City.

D1311258

For Anne and Vincent, Isis and Mandisa – M.H.

For Kenneth, Gwen, Nanette
and their families – C.V.W. and Y.H.

First published in Great Britain in 1997 by
Frances Lincoln Children's Books, 4 Torriano Mews,
Torriano Avenue, London NW5 2RZ
www.franceslincoln.com

This paperback edition published in the USA in 2007

British Library Cataloguing in Publication Data available on request

ISBN 978-1-84507-733-4

Illustrated with watercolors

Set in Fairfield LH Medium

Printed in China

1 3 5 7 9 8 6 4 2

An Angel
Just Like Me

MARY HOFFMAN

Illustrated by
CORNELIUS VAN WRIGHT & YING-HWA HU

F

FRANCES LINCOLN
CHILDREN'S BOOKS

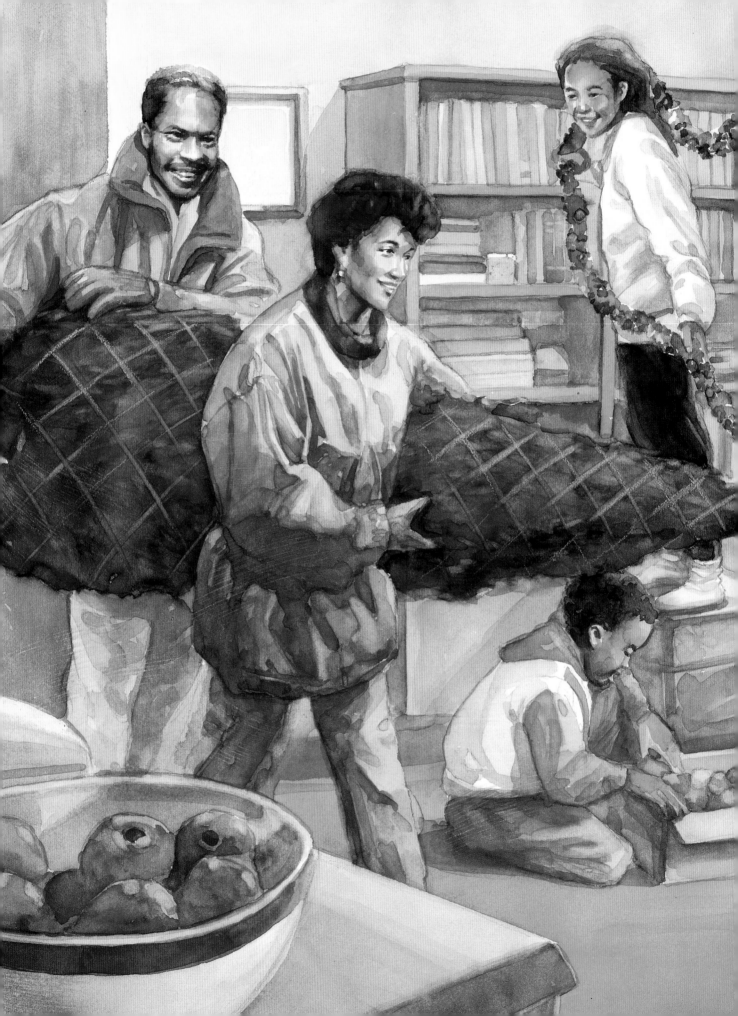

It was nearly Christmas, and everyone in the family was busy except for Tyler. Labelle and Marcy were putting up holly and ivy. Their mother and father were bringing in a big Christmas tree, and T.J. was sorting through the old box of decorations. Even Simone was sticking paper chains together. Tyler was the only one with nothing to do, so he teased Muffin.

"Oh no," said T.J. after a while. "Look at this angel!"

Everyone stopped what they were doing and looked at the angel. It was broken in half.

"We'll have to get a new one," sighed Mom.

Tyler picked it up. "Why do angels all look like girls?" he asked. "Can't boys be angels?"

But no one answered. "Why do they all have gold hair?" asked Tyler. "And why are they always pink? Aren't there any black angels?"

"Good question," said Dad. "There may be, but I've never seen one."

"I'm going to find one," announced Tyler. "I'm going to get a new angel for our tree. One that looks just like me."

Now that Tyler had a special job, he worked hard at it. Every day after school he went shopping and looked at angels. Some were big and some were small, some had straight hair and some had curls. They all had wings. But Tyler couldn't find one that looked like him.

And another thing—none of the angels on the Christmas cards or wrapping paper looked like him either. Some played beautiful gold harps and trumpets. Some perched on rooftops or lolled on clouds. But Tyler couldn't find a single one that looked like him.

Tyler thought maybe Santa Claus could help. At Fogelman's there was a Santa Claus with curly white hair and a beard and red cheeks that matched his clothes, but Tyler thought he couldn't be the real one. Somehow, Tyler had always imagined that Santa Claus might look a little like his own dad.

Just as Tyler was turning away, another Santa came to take over. This one wore his beard like shaving cream on his brown face. He had a huge stomach. Tyler poked him.

"Hi, Carl," he said. "Is that stomach all yours?"

"Hi, Tyler," said the Santa. "No, it's a cushion. But you're not supposed to recognize me. This is my holiday job."

Carl was an art student who was sometimes the children's sitter when Mom and Dad both had to work late. Tyler told Carl his problem.

"I see," said Carl. "I never thought about that, but you're right. You *should* be able to find angels like you."

"There's not much time left," said Tyler. "I guess if I can't find my angel, I'll just have to get a star instead. A star's the same for everyone."

On Christmas Eve Tyler's family went to church. Inside there was a Nativity scene with Jesus and His family. Animals, shepherds, and the Three Kings crowded the stable too.

"Hey," said Tyler. "That king looks a lot like you, Dad."

But the angels were just like the ones he had seen in the shops. And something else was beginning to bug Tyler.

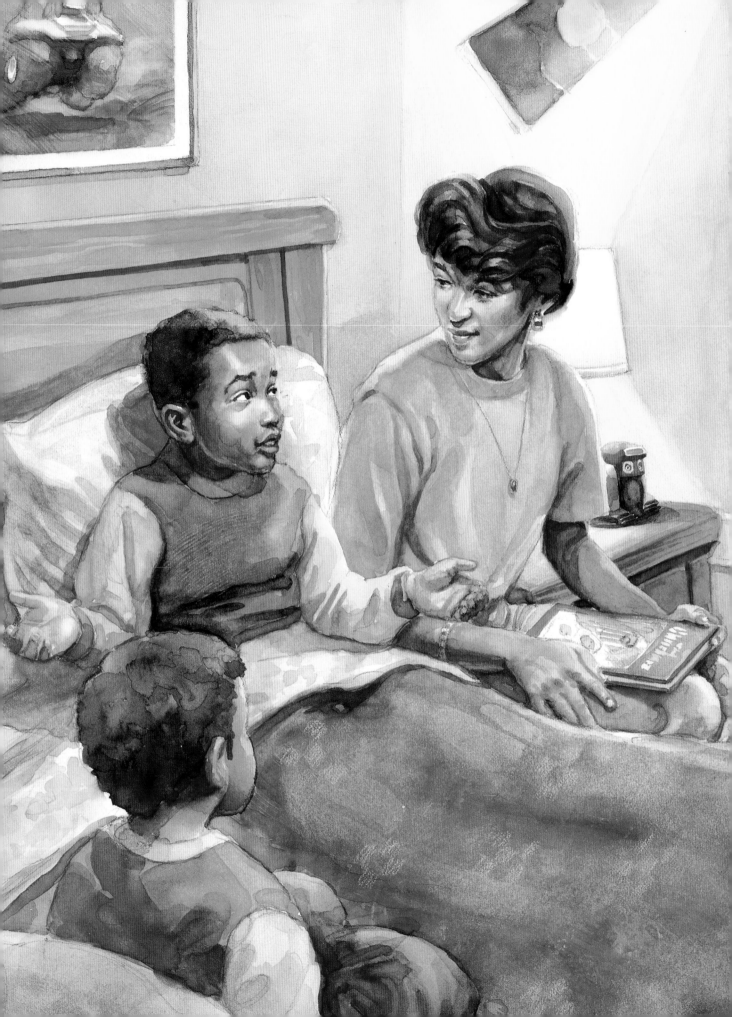

That night, before the children went to sleep, their mother read them the story of the first Christmas again.

"So Jesus was born in Bethlehem, right?" asked Tyler.

"Right," said Mom. "Nearly two thousand years ago."

"And that's in Israel, right?" said Tyler. "And Mary and Joseph were Jewish, right?"

"Right again," said Mom. "Jesus too. They all lived in the Middle East."

"Then why doesn't the baby in the stable at church look Jewish?" asked Tyler. "He had yellow hair."

"Well, you can be Jewish and still have yellow hair," said Mom, but her head was beginning to ache.

"What about two thousand years ago?" persisted Tyler. "What did the baby Jesus really look like?"

"It's a good question," sighed Mom. "You're full of them this Christmas. But I don't know the answers. And if you don't go to sleep now, tomorrow's question is going to be, 'Where's our Christmas dinner?' Good night, Tyler."

On the other side of town Santa Claus was working late.

Christmas day was always special at Tyler's house. There were two grandmas and one grandpa, an aunt and three cousins, and even a visiting dog for Muffin to play with. It was as crowded as the stable in church. Tyler looked up at the brand-new gold star on the top of the tree and gave a little sigh.

"Stars are good," said Dad. "They are the same for everyone."

"Yes," said Tyler, "but you can see stars in the sky almost any night. They're not as special as angels."

At that moment Mom walked in with a package.

"Late delivery from Santa," she told Tyler. "This just came for you."

It was the most beautifully carved wooden angel. And—apart from the wings—it looked just like Tyler.

The next day Tyler went to see Carl and invite him back to share all the food that was left over from Christmas dinner.

"It was my best present," he told Carl. "Only now I want you to make something else."

"OK," said Carl. "What is it?"

"You see," said Tyler, "now that my friends have seen my angel, they all want . . .

. . . angels just like them!"